A Katy and Friends Adventure

Hidden Treasures
in
Grandma's Attic

Illustrator
Britanny Zendejas

BROWN BOOKS KIDS

Tom Frazee

Hidden Treasures in Grandma's Attic

Brown Books Kids
16250 Knoll Trail Drive, Suite 205
Dallas, Texas 75248
www.BrownBooks.com
(972) 381-0009

A New Era in Publishing®

ISBN 978-1-61254-873-9
LCCN 2016930864

Printed in the United States
10 9 8 7 6 5 4 3 2 1

For more information or to contact the author, please go to www.KatyAndFriends.com.

For my wife, Elaine, the inspiration for this book and the creator and technical director of a corresponding children's ballet titled *Hidden Treasures in Grandma's Attic*.

Table of Contents

Introduction

Set in the 1890s, this book and corresponding children's ballet offer an exciting, fun-filled, and at times suspenseful story for readers and viewers. Both introduce the main character, a young, redheaded girl named Katy, along with her family and five friends, who come together for a debutante ball in a small, rural county. They draw readers and viewers back to the slower-paced days of the horse and buggy, when family values and close friendships were expected, enjoyed, and cherished.

Cast of Characters

The Kelleys: Mother, Father, Katy, and Katy's older sister, Elise

Grandma and Grandpa

Mary Porter and her older sister, Emma

Minnie Rockdale and her older sister, Martha

Ruth Grayson and her older sister, Anna

Lilly Hobart and her older sister, Sarah

Helen Riddell and her older sister, Beth

Housekeeping and kitchen girls

Midnight and Storm, Father's horses

Ben and Molly, Grandpa's horses

Horace, the big brown box turtle

Ghost, Grandma's cat

Cadet Colonel Hargrove from Rickson Military Academy

Cadet Carter from Rickson Military Academy

Excitement on the Trip to Grandma's House

The fall day had arrived chilly and windy, and Mother insisted we wear warm clothes for our trip to Grandma's house. Father had hitched our two spirited horses—Midnight, who was black as night, and Storm, who was white as snow—to our covered buggy for the long trip over some winding and rocky roads. After ensuring all our bags had been securely tied to the rear of the buggy, Father called out, "Hurry up, everyone, we need to get going. Grandma's expecting us, and tonight's a very special night for Elise." My mother, my older sister, Elise, and I—my name's Katy, and we're the Kelleys—came out of the house, quickly climbed into the buggy, and pulled blankets over our laps. With a gentle snap of the reins, Father started the team up the gravel road away from our old redbrick-and-stone farmhouse.

The inside of our buggy was a bit snug with Father on the front seat and Mother, Elise, and I on the back seat, but it was peaceful. The only sounds were the clip-clopping of Midnight and Storm's hooves on the rocky road and the chirping of songbirds, which seemed to be singing just for us. Bumping and swaying along, we could see trees on both sides of the road that were brightly painted in reds, yellows, greens, and browns. As they fell, the leaves danced and swirled in a confused flight against the blue and cloudless sky. I snuggled deeper under my blanket to keep warm and looked forward to our stay with Grandma.

Grandma's house, by the way, was the largest in Rickson County.

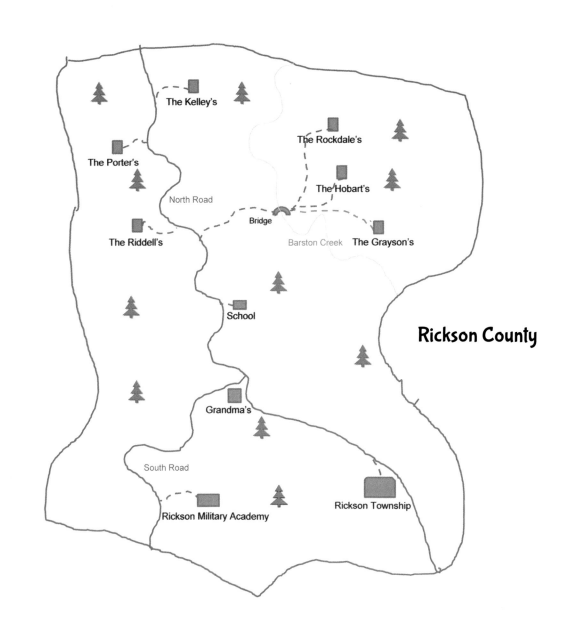

The Kelley's

The Rockdale's

The Porter's

The Hobart's

North Road

The Riddell's

Bridge

Barston Creek

The Grayson's

School

Rickson County

Grandma's

South Road

Rickson Military Academy

Rickson Township

Each year, Grandma opened the doors of her big old house to family, friends, neighbors, and cadets from a nearby military academy for the county's annual debutante ball. It was one of the county's biggest events of the year, and people from near and far were invited to attend. While those invited had the opportunity to enjoy Grandma's hospitality for the evening, she offered debutantes and their families a special invitation to stay overnight in her home after the ball. This year, six debutantes were being honored, and six families would be staying overnight with Grandma, including my family.

It was obvious that my older sister, Elise, was having a hard time sitting still in our bouncing buggy. She was sixteen and more excited than I'd ever seen her. Over the past month, she'd told me over and over that she could not wait to have Father formally introduce her at the debutante ball. Because of the ball that evening, Elise was nearly jumping up and down with excitement in the seat next to me. A debutante ball was apparently a big deal, as it was something Mother called a rite of passage for young ladies.

Mother said that after tonight's ball, Elise would be viewed as an adult and would be eligible to marry a suitable young man of her choosing. *"Yuck,"* I quietly whispered to myself.

Elise and Mother had searched for a dress for Elise to wear at the debutante ball and finally ordered one from the Sears, Roebuck & Company catalog. It had arrived several weeks ago and was now carefully packed in a hard-sided bag closely guarded at Elise's feet. It was fun to watch her reach down and touch the bag. I wasn't sure if she was being overly protective of the bag . . . *Ha* . . . or if she just wanted to reach inside to feel her new dress. *Phooey!*

Elise wasn't the only one excited to get to Grandma's. I was, too! While it was difficult sitting still on the buggy's hard seat while we bounced down a rocky road, my mind was focused on seeing Grandma and Grandpa, spending the evening with my friends, and exploring the nooks and crannies in Grandma's house and barn.

Suddenly, Midnight and Storm spooked and reared onto their hind legs, causing the buggy to bounce wildly. Mother and Elise screamed and grabbed onto the buggy's rails while Father shouted at the horses. He quickly got them under control and brought the buggy to a sudden stop. I looked out the side of the buggy and realized the horses had been startled by a big brown box turtle that had unfortunately decided to cross the road at the exact same time we were riding by.

Without asking, I jumped out of the buggy, my red hair flying in every direction, and scooped up the turtle. I looked up at Father with an expectant look on my freckled face and said, "May I please keep the turtle, Father? I've already named him Horace." I could see the hint of a smile on his face, but I knew that he wasn't very happy with the prospect of another animal about to be added to my menagerie back home.

Father turned to Mother, and she slowly nodded her head with a knowing look. Father finally smiled and said, "OK, Katy. You may keep Horace, but you know it's your responsibility to take care of him."

With a shout of happiness, I said, "I will!" and climbed back into the buggy. Leaning down, I bunched up my blanket on the floorboards under my seat and carefully set Horace inside. I sat back up, Father clucked softly to the horses, and off we went. I could tell that Midnight and Storm were skittish and prancing somewhat uneasily, not knowing what they might encounter crossing the road around the next turn. Looking under my seat, I saw that Horace was snuggled in the folds of my blanket and had already fallen fast asleep.

2

Apples and Carrots for Ben and Molly

Mother, Elise, and I chattered most of the way on the long buggy ride to Grandma's. Father was a quiet man and drove the buggy in silence, only talking and calling out to our edgy horses to keep them under control. I was sure that he was looking forward to spending time with Grandpa and the other fathers. It seemed like you could always find them standing in the side yard under Grandma's big elm tree or on the porch, smoking their pipes, drinking lemonade, and discussing "father stuff," like cows and crops and combines.

As we rounded a final turn, there sat Grandma's beautiful, white, clapboard-sided, two-story house in the middle of a freshly mowed and very green meadow. Grandpa had obviously been out mowing earlier that week with his two big draft horses, Ben and Molly. They're gentle giants that love apples and carrots, and Mother had agreed that I could bring a small bag of treats from home to give to Ben and Molly.

We could see Grandma waving from her porch steps with a big smile on her face. Grandpa stood next to her, waving as well. They quickly walked down to the edge of the driveway. I couldn't see any other buggies in Grandma's drive and realized we were the first to arrive. From her big smile, I could see that Grandma was as happy to see us as we were to see her. Pulling into the drive, Father called out, "Whoa," to the horses, and they came to a stop at the foot of Grandma's front steps. I jumped down and ran into Grandma's open arms. She wore an apron over her housedress that was dusted here and there with flour. She smelled like a mix of freshly baked cookies, sweet jam, and the lingering fragrance of Grandpa's cherry-blend pipe tobacco.

In one very long breath, I quickly told Grandma about our wild ride, how the horses had spooked at the sight of my new pet turtle, Horace, and that I'd brought apples and carrots for Ben and Molly. Still smiling, Grandma hugged me tightly and said, "My goodness, Katy, you've had quite an adventure on your drive here. I'm so glad you're safe and sound, and I'm so happy you've come to visit. We'll talk more later, but if you'll excuse me, I want to say hello to your mother and father."

As Grandma turned to speak to Mother and Father, I hugged Grandpa and repeated everything I'd told Grandma. "Sounds like you've had some real excitement this morning," Grandpa said. "Why don't we go see Ben and Molly now? I'm sure they'll be happy to see you."

I quickly got the bag of apples and carrots out of the buggy. Hand in hand, Grandpa and I headed for the barn to go see . . . oh, heck . . . to spoil Ben and Molly.

3

Friends Meeting Friends

Hearing a commotion, Grandpa and I quickly walked back from the barn to the front of the house after feeding Ben and Molly their treats. We saw five buggies full of grinning and excited families in Grandma's drive. In the first buggy were the Porters, and I watched as Elise hugged her friend Emma as she stepped from the buggy. Together they ran to the next buggy, which held the Rockdales, and greeted another debutante, Martha. Then all three ran to the other buggies in line to hug their friends Anna Grayson, Sarah Hobart, and Beth Riddell.

I smiled up at Grandpa and said, "Thanks for taking me out to see Ben and Molly, Grandpa, but if you don't mind, I'd like to go say hello to my friends." He smiled and motioned me toward the buggies with a wave of his pipe, which swirled smoky trails here and there. "Thank you, Grandpa," I said. Now it was my turn. I ran to the first buggy to hug my friend Mary Porter as she jumped down. Mary and I ran to the other buggies and hugged Minnie Rockdale, Ruth Grayson, Lilly Hobart, and Helen Riddell as they got out of their buggies. We were all ten years old and had been friends forever. Although we were together during the week at school, it was a special treat for us to spend an entire night together. My friends and I agreed to meet in the kitchen right after we helped our fathers finish unpacking our buggies.

Mother and Grandma chatted while Father and I untied the bags and began carrying them toward the house. Elise hurried past us, carefully cradling the bag with her dress in her arms. She opened the door for Father and me and then ran past us up the stairs to one of Grandma's guest bedrooms on the right side of the hall.

This was the bedroom we always used when visiting Grandma. It was much bigger than the one Elise and I shared back home. It had two big beds covered in colorful quilts, a dresser, a mirror, and a tall, open window that looked out over Grandma's circular drive. Father and I put down our bags and began unpacking as Elise placed the bag with her dress onto the bed farthest from the door.

I watched as she undid the bag's clasps to take a peek at her dress. She and Mother had been so careful packing it. The Sears, Roebuck & Company catalog had said that the material was white *peau de soie* silk, whatever that was, but the dress was smooth and satiny and had lace at the neck and cuffs. *Phooey!*

Elise gave a sigh of relief and said, "I'm so happy my dress made the trip safely. I wonder if one of the handsome and dashing cadets will notice me tonight at the ball?"

Yuck!

Elise then carefully closed her bag and ran back down the front stairs to meet her friends at Grandma's old glider swing. Sitting three across, they glided back and forth, their conversation likely lingering on dresses, the night's festivities, and the expectation of meeting and dancing with some of the handsome young cadets from Rickson Academy.

After helping Father unpack the bags, I hurried back out to the barn and found a small wooden box on a shelf near the wall where Grandpa kept his tools. I filled the bottom of the box with freshly mowed grass that I found in the meadow near the barn and walked back to our buggy. "Horace," I said, "wake up. I have a nice, soft place for you to stay while we're here at Grandma's." I gently picked him up and placed him inside the box on top of the soft, green grass.

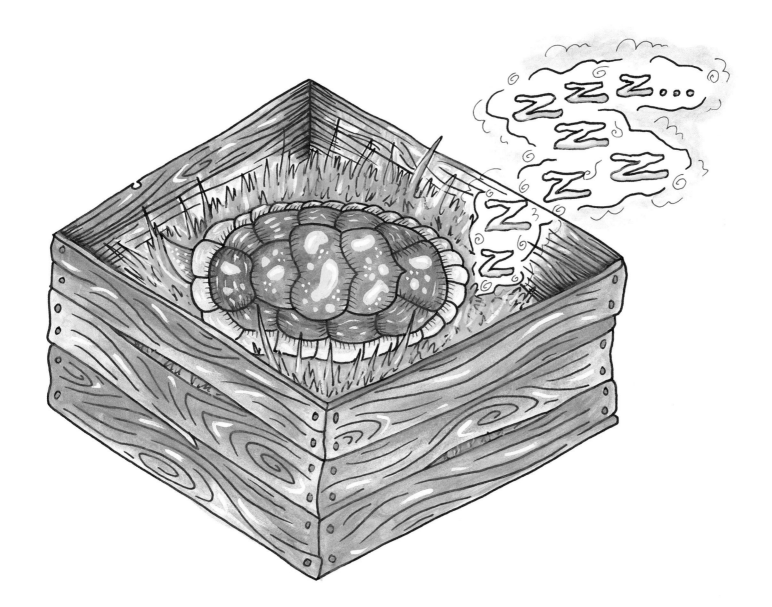

Looking down, I saw that he never even woke up. I guessed Horace was a heavy sleeper. With his box in my arms, I went to find my friends and found them coming down the front steps from Grandma's second floor, where they, too, had been helping their fathers with their family's bags.

To my surprise, Horace woke up. Standing in the entry hall, each of my friends reached in and petted his hard, brown shell. Instead of being frightened and pulling his head inside, Horace confidently craned his neck to look at each of them, seeming to offer a silent, "Glad to meet you, and thank you for patting my shell." I quickly took Horace up the stairs to my parents' bedroom and found a place for the box in a corner. I came back down, and the six of us walked into Grandma's kitchen, where we found a special surprise waiting for us on the table. We sat, ate fresh cookies, drank ice-cold milk, and talked and talked about the exciting evening ahead.

Later, Grandma came into the kitchen and smiled at the empty plate of cookies and looks of contentment on our faces. In a kind voice, she said, "Katy, I think it's time for me to show you and your friends where you'll be sleeping tonight. Would you like that?"

In unison, we all said, "Yes!"

We followed Grandma up the back stairs from the kitchen and past the second floor, where we saw our mothers standing in the hall, talking and laughing. I stepped into my parents' room and quickly gathered Horace, still cozy inside his box, into my arms. We then began walking up the steep stairs that led to the attic. The stairs were narrow, and the way was a bit dark, but when Grandma opened a large door at the top of the stairs, we found ourselves standing in the middle of Grandma's huge attic. I quickly took Horace's box and placed it in one of the attic's dim corners.

As we gawked at the size of the attic, Grandma said, "As you know, your mothers, fathers, and older sisters are staying on the second floor tonight. You'll be sleeping up here in my special attic, and I have no doubt that you'll have a wonderful time exploring. The cadets, who are joining us from Rickson Military Academy, will be staying in the barn."

No sooner had Grandma finished speaking than we heard singing coming from down the south road. My friends and I ran to the small, open window at the end of the attic and saw a large, high-sided farm wagon pulled by two huge Missouri mules with big, pointy ears coming up the road toward Grandma's drive. On the high-mounted seat at the front of the wagon sat two older men in long, dusty coats. In the back, on benches along the sides of the wagon bed, sat eight young men—also in long, dusty coats—who apparently were the cadets from Rickson Military Academy. The cadets sat straight as ramrods on their wagon benches. As they got closer, we could just hear the last few lines of their school song:

"Defend our country, brave men of war,
Fight for victory and never yield,
We honor our academy as part of the Corps,
We'll always stand tall on the battlefield!"

4

Rickson Military Academy Cadets Arrive for the Ball

The cadets finished singing as the driver pulled hard on the reins to direct the mules into Grandma's drive. From a window below us, we could hear our older sisters sighing loudly. We listened as they babbled about how cute the cadets were and wondered if they were all good dancers. We even heard one of our older sisters say that she hoped they were good kissers.

Double yuck!

We watched as Grandpa and our fathers, who had been standing in the side yard near the front porch, each with a cold cup of lemonade in his hand, talking, turned toward the arriving wagon of cadets. Grandpa walked out of the side yard and down to the drive to greet the academy's officers and cadets. The wagon drove smartly into the drive and came to a stop right in front of him. With a smile, Grandpa said, "Welcome, Colonel. I'm glad you and your cadets could make our special event again this year. As you know, the debutantes and

their families will be staying here in the house, and you and your cadets will be staying in the barn. We've already got bowls and pitchers full of fresh water set up for you so that you can freshen up. We've also set up cots with blankets on them in the back of the barn for you to use later tonight. Make yourselves at home. Just to let you know, Grandma will be serving dinner at six out in the backyard. You don't want to miss that."

"Thank you for inviting us," Cadet Colonel Hargrove replied. "We've been looking forward to your event for months. I must admit that I especially have been looking forward to Grandma's wonderful food and her delicious sweet cakes and cookies." Colonel Hargrove then nodded at the other officer driving the team, who gently snapped the reins, and the wagon slowly started to make the turn around the drive heading toward the barn. Peeking out from the window in the attic, we could see canvas haversacks tied to the back of the wagon, which likely held the uniforms the cadets would be wearing at tonight's ball.

As we stepped back from the window, Grandma told us she needed to speak to her housekeeping and kitchen staff to make sure that everything was ready for this evening's activities. "Have a wonderful time this afternoon and this evening," she said with a loving smile. She then walked back down the stairs to the first floor and into the parlor, where she found three young housekeeping girls with brooms in their hands, three others with feather dusters, and three kitchen girls with dishrags.

Grandma said to the staff, "Tonight's a big night for all of us, and I want it to be extra special for the debutantes, for their families, and for our friends, our neighbors, and the cadets. I'm relying on each of you to be sure that this parlor is clean and tidy, since there will be a lot of dancing *and* eating in here tonight. It's important that you housekeeping girls work with the kitchen staff to be sure that all of the dishes, silverware, and glasses we're putting out for our guests are clean and neatly arranged on the tables here in the parlor."

Grandma slowly turned her head, looking intently at the girls to be sure each had heard her and understood how important this evening's ball was to her. Each of them knew that Grandma had carefully planned every aspect of the evening's activities, including the preparation of delicious food as well as cakes and cookies for her guests. They knew she wanted the parlor to be spick and span, with all of the serving pieces clean and sparkling, and to be sure that all the goodies that had been prepared were out and readily available to her guests. The nine girls looked straight at Grandma and solemnly nodded their heads. They weren't going to disappoint her on this special night.

Grandma smiled at them and said, "As you can hear, our houseguests have already arrived, and I'm expecting friends and neighbors to begin arriving just before dinnertime. Your jobs are important. Please be sure to extend every courtesy to our guests."

After giving the housekeeping and kitchen girls their final instructions, Grandma walked over to a sideboard cabinet and pulled open one of the doors. She reached in and, to their surprise, took out a plate of freshly baked cookies and offered them to the girls. Smelling the wonderful aroma of Grandma's famous cookies, the girls pressed forward, each taking one from the plate. After everyone had enjoyed several cookies, Grandma sent them off so that they could continue with their final preparations for the evening's activities.

Exploring Grandma's Farm

The afternoon passed quickly as my friends and I explored the farm. Out in the barn, we named each of the cows and every one of the pigs and sprinkled far too many kernels of corn for the chickens clucking and strutting in the barnyard. We even spotted a light-brown field mouse just before it ducked back into a hole in the barn's weathered siding.

The mouse's sudden departure was likely due to the appearance of Grandma's gray-striped cat, Ghost. The cat nosed at the small hole into which the mouse had disappeared. Realizing the mouse had gotten away, Ghost turned with a dejected look and walked slowly back out of the barn.

To our delight, we heard a clanging bell from the backyard announcing dinner was being served. As we came around the house from the barn, we saw that all of Grandma's guests had arrived and were sitting either at picnic tables or on blankets scattered across the backyard.

Grandma's kitchen staff had brought out platters of fried chicken they had spent hours frying in hot, bubbling oil in large cast-iron skillets. The platters of steaming-hot chicken were sitting in the center of Grandma's serving table. Alongside the fried chicken, Grandma had pans of golden-brown biscuits and freshly churned butter; thickly sliced roast beef sandwiches on homemade bread; bowls of vegetables; pitchers of milk, tea, and coffee; and large metal platters overflowing with raisin and nut crumble and cinnamon and sugar delight cookies. Standing in line as we waited to fill our plates, my friends and I could hardly wait to dig into the feast that Grandma and her staff had prepared, especially her wonderful cookies.

After filling their plates, the debutantes sat together at one of the wooden picnic tables while my friends and I sat at another. We rolled our eyes as they continued to sneak peeks at the cadets, who were sitting on the grass with heaping plates of food on their laps. Our older sisters had expected the cadets to be peeking over at them but were disappointed that the cadets were obviously more interested in Grandma's cooking. "Don't worry," I heard Elise say. "They'll notice us this evening at the ball."

Phooey! When everyone had finally finished, Grandma called out to my friends and me and said, "Katy, would you and your friends please help me clean up out here in the yard while your sisters go upstairs with your mothers to get ready for the ball?" Knowing that we weren't invited to the ball and that, following dinner, we were headed for Grandma's attic, we agreed to help pick up the dirty dishes and trash.

When we began bringing the dirty dishes, cups, and silverware into the kitchen, we saw that the staff already had the huge, white, porcelain-covered cast-iron sink filled nearly to overflowing with sudsy water and were washing the many pots and pans from the meal. A stack of clean pots and pans sat drying on the sink's large drain board.

Running back and forth into the kitchen with dirty dishes, my friends and I couldn't help but notice a leftover platter of cookies that Grandma or one of the kitchen girls had placed on a counter in the far corner of the kitchen.

Cookie Mishap

When all the dishes had been brought inside and all the trash placed in a large barrel that Grandpa had placed next to the back door, Grandma shooed us upstairs to the attic. We reluctantly walked up the back stairs from the kitchen to the second floor, where we found our mothers and sisters frantically getting ready for the ball. Evening had arrived, and flames flickered in the kerosene lamps that hung in the second-floor hallway. From the parlor below, we could hear fiddlers beginning to tune up their instruments for the ball.

As you might imagine, standing there in the back hallway on the second floor of Grandma's, we were torn. We knew we weren't invited to the ball and had been told to go on up to the attic for the night. Even so, we really wanted to take a peek at the festivities in the parlor. More importantly, though, we wanted some of those cookies that were on that metal tray on the counter in the far corner of Grandma's kitchen.

Finally ready, our mothers and sisters rushed down the front stairs to the parlor. We looked at each other and, with mischievous grins, turned and crept down the back stairs to the kitchen.

Much to our delight, after it had been so busy just a short time ago, we could see that the kitchen was now quiet and empty since everyone had gone into the parlor for the start of the ball. The kitchen staff and housekeeping girls had also left the kitchen, *and* they'd left that big platter of cookies—just for us, of course. Slipping silently into the kitchen, we walked to the far corner and sadly realized that Grandma's counters were a bit higher than we had expected. Still, we wanted those cookies. So, standing on our tiptoes, Minnie and I reached up and began pulling the cookie platter off the high counter. Apparently, we tugged a bit too hard, and without warning, the platter began to slide quickly off the counter toward us.

There was a huge crash as the platter of cookies tumbled down onto Minnie and me. All of us were alarmed by the loud noise and the mess we'd made. We stood very still, wondering who would come to investigate the crash. Without thinking, I said, "Quick, grab as many cookies as you can." Even though we were scared, we each scrambled to put a cookie into our mouth and stuffed another into our pocket.

Not surprisingly, the sound of the crashing platter had alerted eagle-ears Beth Riddell and my sister, Elise, and they came running into the kitchen in their ball dresses to see what had happened. Helen and I looked at each other and rolled our eyes; we knew it was likely to be our nosy sisters who would come to investigate. Beth and Elise were none too happy with the mess we'd made. In stern tones, they told us we were interrupting their special night and that we needed to clean up the mess on the floor and get back upstairs to the attic.

When our two older sisters had run into the kitchen, we had all turned toward them and stood closely side by side; everyone, that is, except Ruth Grayson. She had found a large cloth napkin in one of the kitchen drawers and was down on her hands and knees behind us, stashing as many cookies as she could into that napkin. With the last of the cookies safely inside, Ruth tied the napkin, stood up, and quietly put the bundle of cookies onto the counter. She slowly turned back toward Beth and Elise with a look of absolute innocence on her face.

Minnie ran to get a dustpan and small brush, and we quickly cleaned up the remaining mess. In a firm but gentle voice, Elise said, "Your sisters and I have waited a long time for this evening's activities. Tonight's ball is in our honor, but each of you will be a debutante in a few years and will have your own ball. Right now, it's time for you to go back upstairs to the attic."

When Helen began to pout and whine, Beth grabbed her younger sister by the back of her dress and began to pull her none too gently toward the back stairs. With a collective sigh of disappointment since we could hear music and happy voices coming from the nearby parlor, we trudged back up to Grandma's attic.

Oh, yes; as we all turned to begin that walk back up the stairs, Ruth carefully and slyly slipped the tied napkin off the counter and held it closely in front of her. Our two older sisters followed us up the faintly lit stairs to be sure that we made it up to the attic "safely."

7

Wrapped Up in Blankets and Sharing Cookies

With that small window wide open, we found the temperature a bit chilly as we walked into the dim attic. Grandma had lit two kerosene lamps, which blazed cheerfully through slightly blackened glass chimneys as they sat on empty wooden nail kegs in the center of the attic. To be sure we'd stay warm, our mothers had brought each of us a big blanket up to the attic that we were to use for sleeping. On our blankets, they had also laid our rag dolls. Hugging our dolls, we wrapped the blankets around ourselves. At the older sisters' urging, we reluctantly curled up on the floor.

But as I said, it was still early in the evening, and we certainly weren't sleepy. Mary and I popped up from our blankets and were firmly told by Elise and Beth to lie back down. As we unwillingly did so, Minnie and Ruth popped up, and they were told, more sternly, to lie back down. As you might imagine, Lilly and Helen, not to be outdone, then popped up and said, "We're just not sleepy, and we want to go to the ball."

Elise and Beth patiently shook their heads, said no, and then carefully tucked us back into our blankets. They again reminded us that, in a few years, we would be the guests of honor at our own debutante ball.

As we watched from under our blankets, Elise and Beth danced around the two lamps in the center of the attic to a tune that was drifting up from the parlor below. Seeing us watching them, they gave us a withering look, turned, and ran back down the stairs to their exciting and memorable debutante ball.

From the parlor below, snippets of melodies and laughter drifted up to the attic. We were having a difficult time staying up there with all the fun going on down in the parlor. With nothing better to do, we talked about all that was happening in our lives and on our farms. Every once in a while, we'd stop talking and look toward the stairs. You know, it just wasn't fair that we'd been told to go to sleep so early in the evening with a noisy party and delicious treats downstairs.

We agreed that when the time came for us to have our own debutante ball, we'd make our older sisters go to bed early in the evening right here in the attic. Curled up in our blankets, we could hear the buzzing and chirping of night bugs and crickets down in the yard. Ruth untied her napkin of "rescued" cookies, and we happily munched on them.

The persistent buzzing and chirping provided a pleasant background as we laid back and talked about what our debutante ball would be like and described to one another the beautiful dresses we'd be wearing in a few short years.

8

Finding Hidden Treasures in Grandma's Attic

As the last song ended some time later, the debutante ball drew to a close. All of the guests walked out to the front yard and stood talking and saying their good-byes. The debutantes sadly walked back upstairs to the second floor. Their special evening was over.

Grandma quickly assembled her housekeeping and kitchen staff in the parlor and quietly said, "It's been a wonderful evening, and each of you has done a fine job. But now we have a lot of cleanup to do, and I want everything cleaned and back in its place before you head off to bed."

With that, the girls with brooms and girls with feather dusters nodded to Grandma and quickly went about cleaning the parlor and entry hall. The kitchen staff again filled the big old sink with sudsy water and began cleaning all the dishes, cups, and silverware from the ball. One girl washed, and the other two dried. "How many dishes did they use?" asked one of the girls, drying the mountain of plates and cups.

Back up in Grandma's attic, my friends and I had listened to the music fade away and realized the ball was finally over. Each of us was still far too excited and definitely not ready to go to sleep. "Let's explore Grandma's attic," I said, munching on one of the last of the cookies from Ruth's napkin. Leaving my blanket on the floor, I picked up one of the kerosene lamps, and the other girls stood up with me. Like great explorers, we began to search the attic.

I was the first to spy a big old wooden trunk with a rounded top, rusty hinges, and an unlocked hasp that had been pushed back into a dim corner of the attic. Jabbering with excitement about what might be inside, we gathered around the trunk, but we were reluctant to touch it, much less open it.

"This is your grandma's house, Katy," Minnie whispered. "I'm sure it would be all right if you opened the trunk."

All my friends looked at me and nodded.

I gulped, reluctantly said, *"OK,"* and handed the lamp to Lilly. I pulled open the old, ornate hasp and attempted to lift the lid. It was way too heavy for me. Helen and Mary came to help, and together we lifted the lid. Because of its rusty hinges, the lid squeaked loudly, and several of the girls yelped in fright. We all looked toward the stairs to see if anyone had heard the squeaking sound and would be coming to investigate. When no one came running up the stairs, we all let out a sigh of relief. Helen, Mary, and I turned back to the trunk and pushed the lid completely open so that it was leaning against the attic's rafters.

Lilly raised the lamp high over the open trunk as each of us pressed forward to get a look at what treasures might be inside. Wanting to explore the trunk with us, Lilly moved an empty nail keg over next to the trunk and carefully placed the lamp onto it.

Together, we all began digging down into the trunk. It was definitely full of treasures. There were old shirts and jackets, old serving dishes, some colorful flags, and even some old corsets. Mary, Ruth, and I grabbed some large, floppy hats with bent feathers in the hat bands and promptly put them on our heads. Minnie, Lilly, and Helen found funny-looking dress hoops like those our mothers wore under their wide dresses. Mary, Ruth, and I helped the others by unsnapping the hooks on the hoops, putting the hoops around our friends' waists, and then re-snapping the hooks.

There we stood in our big, floppy hats and funny-looking dress hoops. Minnie said, "I have an idea. Let's have our own ball." We thought that was a great idea and began to dance around the attic. We waltzed and twirled for what seemed like a very long time until finally, so tired, we plopped down onto the attic's wooden floor back in one dim corner.

I was drifting off to sleep when I heard a soft thumping noise. Mary, wide-eyed and scared, shook my shoulder and pointed at the stairs. "Someone's coming!" she whispered.

We all huddled together as the thumping noise grew louder.

9

Housekeeping Girls Invade Grandma's Attic

At that very moment, two of the housekeeping girls with their feather dusters came up the stairs from the second floor. They were chattering quietly and were totally unaware of us sitting on the floor in a dark corner of the attic. To our delight, we watched as they pretended to powder each other's nose with their feather dusters, likely copying our mothers and older sisters while they prepared for the ball. With quiet laughter, they linked arms and began to do a cancan dance, kicking their feet up higher and higher. But their "powdering" had tickled their noses with dust, and they began sneezing as they danced. In a fit of giggles, they plopped down onto the attic floor, tired from their dancing.

A small noise, however, alerted the housekeeping girls that they weren't alone in the nearly dark attic. On our hands and knees, my friends and I had quietly encircled them. Together, we jumped up and said, "Boo!" The housekeeping girls yelped in fear and just sat there with their mouths open, surprised and scared.

With a stern look, Helen waggled her finger at them and said, "I wonder if Grandma knows you're up here in the attic? You're probably supposed to be in the parlor cleaning. And here you are in the attic, dancing and playing. Naughty, naughty."

Hearing this, the housekeeping girls looked ashamed and remained silent, staring at the floor. For some reason, I turned back toward the trunk and saw the two large corsets we'd found earlier now lying on the floor. I picked them up and handed one to Mary, Lilly, and Helen. Minnie, Ruth, and I took the other. Circling around the housekeeping girls, we quickly laced the corsets around them.

As you might imagine, the housekeeping girls were *not* happy about this, but there was nothing they could do about it. They chose not to shout out, as they didn't want Grandma to know where they were and, more importantly, that they weren't cleaning like they were supposed to.

Standing them up, we began pulling the corset laces around each of them. With each tug, the corsets became tighter and tighter, and soon the housekeeping girls were groaning and complaining that they were about to collapse from lack of air. We kept on pulling until both housekeepers began to swoon, the backs of their hands pressed melodramatically against their foreheads. Realizing that the tight corsets might cause the housekeeping girls to lose consciousness, we stopped pulling on the cords and instead started spinning them around and around. It was no surprise when they finally fell into our arms.

Laughing, we gently removed the corsets and pulled the girls to the stairs, heading down to the second floor and carefully placing their feather dusters in their hands. We quickly went back to our blankets in one of the attic's dim corners and covered our heads. None of us had any doubt that we had just made two housekeeping girls very unhappy with us.

10

Not Quite Dancing with Our Big Sisters

A short time later, as we were lying quietly under our blankets, we heard noisy laughter erupt from down the stairs. For a while, we thought the two housekeeping girls had returned. Instead, it was all of our older sisters coming up the stairs into the attic, still dressed in their beautiful ball gowns. Apparently, the housekeeping girls had recovered and disappeared before our sisters came up the stairs. Our older sisters looked over to be sure that we were under our blankets and then turned away and began slowly waltzing around the attic in the dim light of the two kerosene lamps.

While they were slowly dancing, we slipped out of our blankets and sat out of sight with our backs against the trunk to watch. I could see that Elise had a beautiful red rose that she lovingly clutched to her heart. They stopped their slow dancing and, standing in the center of the attic, each spoke quietly and happily about the evening, their many dances with the cadets, and how much fun they'd had.

When it came to Elise's turn, she spoke in a dreamy voice. "It was such a romantic night. Early in the evening, before the dance had even begun, I saw Carter across the parlor. He's a fourth-year cadet, and he's so very handsome. Our eyes met, and I was surprised and a little nervous when he walked over to me. He gallantly gave me this red rose and asked if he could dance with me for the rest of the evening. Somehow, I said yes, and we danced and danced until our feet hurt. We finally joined others out on the porch with a glass of milk and a plate of cookies. At the end of the evening, before the cadets marched back to the barn, he turned to me, lightly kissed me on the lips, and promised that he would see me again. I thought my heart was going to explode. That was my very first kiss, and I know I'm in love."

To that, all I could quietly say was, *Triple yuuuck.* With sighs of happiness and faraway looks in their eyes, our older sisters again began to waltz around the attic, acting as if they were still dancing with their cadets. Watching from the dim corner against the old trunk, we looked at each other and rolled our eyes. How silly our older sisters were acting. We continued to watch and saw that they were completely distracted with all the memories from this evening's debutante ball.

Quietly standing, we turned and looked back into Grandma's trunk of treasures and found six brightly colored flags on small wooden sticks that had been used at last year's county fair parade. While our older sisters danced dreamily around the center of the attic, I laughingly whispered, "If they can have memories about cadets, so can we." I grabbed a stick with a bright red flag tacked onto it, placed it on my shoulder, and quietly said to my friends, "Forward march." The other five girls grabbed a flag and hoisted it onto their shoulders, and we quietly marched around the back of the attic, being sure to stay far away from our waltzing and extremely preoccupied sisters.

We quickly tired of marching around with our colorful flags, so we sat back down in a darkened corner opposite the trunk and watched our older sisters continue to waltz around the center of the attic. After far too many lovey-dovey comments about cute cadets and how they wanted to marry them . . . *Quadruple yuck!* . . . our older sisters spied the open trunk and ran over to it.

Reaching into Grandma's trunk, Sarah Hobart found six old paper umbrellas: one red, one green, one blue, one yellow, one orange, and one brown. They had been carefully packed away in the trunk from a Chinese New Year celebration several years earlier. Each of our sisters took an umbrella, carefully opened it, and placed it on her shoulder. They made a small circle and began prancing around, gently twirling their umbrellas, laughing softly, and quietly humming a melody that had likely been played at the evening's ball.

Around and around they went, dancing first in one direction and then in the other. I hoped they'd get dizzy from going around and around so many times, but after a while, they just stopped dancing, gently returned the umbrellas to the trunk, and, without any further conversation, slowly made their way back down the stairs. Apparently, they were now worn out and were returning to their rooms to get ready for bed. No doubt they would spend the night dreaming about dancing with handsome cadets.

11

Spooky Rattling in the Dim Attic

After our older sisters walked back down the stairs to the second floor, it suddenly became very quiet in the attic. The sounds of our sisters' steps on the stairs had faded, and we sat against the attic wall in the dim light, quietly thinking scary thoughts about ghosts and spooky characters.

From the open window came a long, loud howl. Several girls stiffened, but I quietly said, "That's only a coyote. We're safe here. There's nothing to be scared about." It became quiet again, and then, all of a sudden, we heard a noise. It was a rattling noise from the other dark corner of the attic near the stairs. As if for protection, we grabbed our blankets and pulled them up over our heads. The quiet rattling continued, and we slowly lowered our blankets and looked at each other. We were scared and unsure of what to do.

"Remember, this is your grandma's house, Katy. It's up to you to find out what's making that rattling sound," Mary said in a very frightened voice.

Great, I thought. *It's my grandma's house, and because of that, I'm the one who has to go across this dark and spooky attic to find out what's making that mysterious rattling sound.* Everyone was looking at me and pointing expectantly at the rattling sound. It was obvious that I'd been chosen to solve the mystery.

I had gigantic goose bumps all over me and really didn't want to go see what was making that scary noise. I'm not sure where I found the courage, but I crept across the attic and saw, against the dark wall by the stairs, a small, round table covered with a tablecloth that spilled down onto the floor. As I got closer, I realized that the rattling noise was coming from underneath the table.

I was scared silly and looked back at my friends. They looked just as scared hiding behind their blankets and continued to point me toward the noise. I turned back and crept closer. I really didn't want to look under that tablecloth, but I continued on toward the rattling sound.

All of a sudden, I began to scream, and then all of my friends were screaming as we watched the small table and cloth begin to slowly rise. I rushed back to my friends in the corner and watched the table rise higher off

the floor. Then, to our absolute horror, the table began turning around in circles and slowly started moving across the floor toward us. We jumped up and began running around the attic with the table chasing after us. We screamed and screamed, but the table kept following us, coming closer and closer.

All of a sudden, there stood Grandma at the top of the stairs with a lamp in her hand. We all crowded behind her as she put up her hand and told the table, "Stop!" The table immediately stopped moving and lowered back down to the floor. Grandma walked over and pulled the cloth up and away from the table. To everyone's surprise, under the table were the two housekeeping girls that we'd squeezed into corsets earlier in the evening. They had returned to the attic to pay us back.

In a firm voice, Grandma sent the housekeeping girls back down the stairs, then turned to us with a big smile and said, "You're safe now, and it's time to go to sleep. Morning will be here before you know it." We each took our turn to thank Grandma and to hug and kiss her goodnight.

As she moved toward the stairs, Grandma took one last look back at us. With a smile, she turned and, with her lamp guiding the way, walked out of the attic and down the stairs. We listened to her footsteps echoing down to the second level and heard her quietly close her bedroom door.

We were all still scared, so Ruth and Helen got the two now-dimmer kerosene lamps off the empty nail kegs, and, staying *very* close together, we searched every corner of the attic to be sure there would be no more surprises. Fortunately, we found none.

12

Magical Hat

We reluctantly crawled back under our blankets and pulled our rag dolls close. It had been a long and exciting day and an even more exciting evening. No sooner had we curled up in our blankets than Mary suddenly stood up and began waltzing around with a cadet who looked strangely like her rag doll. The rest of us jumped out from under our blankets, and soon, we were all waltzing around the attic floor with our own "cadet." We were having so much fun, but then Lilly gave a big yawn; Minnie yawned loudly after her, and then the rest of us began yawning. It was time to get to sleep, and, moving as close to the two kerosene lamps as possible, we again crawled under our blankets.

Just as we were about to doze off, we heard a very soft *scratch, scratch, scratch* on the old, wooden attic floor across the way from us. The soft scratching noise continued, and we could hear it slowly coming toward us. With eyes as big as saucers, we peeked out from our blankets toward the sound of the scratching. In the dim light, we were shocked to see one of the big, floppy hats with a bent yellow feather in its band moving very slowly across the floor toward us.

I screamed and screamed, and my friends quickly joined me.

As if by magic, we heard pounding on the stairs, and Grandma reappeared in her nightgown and cap. All we could do was point at the hat on the floor. She quickly walked over and yanked it up. To our relief, beneath the hat was Horace, who had somehow gotten out of his box, slipped under the big, floppy hat, and begun the slow trek over to see us, probably in search of something to eat. Grandma gently picked Horace up, put him back in his box, and turned to us to say again, "You're safe, and everything is OK. It's time for you to get to sleep."

And that's just what we did. We never even heard Grandma walk back down the stairs.

It's Finally Morning and Time for Breakfast

Early the next morning, a very loud and persistent racket woke us. We jumped up, ran to the open window at the end of the attic, and saw Grandpa's plump leghorn rooster, whose name was Oscar, perched on top of a wooden split-rail fence. Oscar was announcing the start of a new day with very loud cock-a-doodle-doos!

Much relieved after the scary evening before, we all laughed. Rubbing sleep from our eyes, we folded our blankets and headed down the stairs to the kitchen. Delicious smells of frying bacon, pancakes, biscuits, and Grandma's apple streusel coffee cake greeted us as we quickly found a place around her kitchen table. Platters of food sat in the middle of the round table, and we each found our favorites and loaded our plates.

The kitchen girls filled our glasses with ice-cold milk from pitchers and then returned to help out in the dining room, where our parents and older sisters were also having their breakfast.

Through the open kitchen window, we could hear voices coming from the barnyard. Quiet orders were being issued to the cadets as mules were hitched to the large farm wagon for the trip back to Rickson Academy. We could hear the mules softly nickering as they were led out into Grandma's large, circular driveway. Several of us, including Elise, ran to the window in time to see the cadets marching toward the back of the wagon and up the two steps before finding seats on benches along the sides of the wagon bed.

I heard Elise sigh quietly as the handsome young cadet named Carter, who had given her a rose the night before, boarded the wagon. When the cadets were all seated, the cadet colonel closed and latched the wagon's back gate, walked around to the front, and climbed up onto the wide wagon seat. He nodded to the other officer, who clucked at the team of mules, turning them out of Grandma's drive and down toward the south road leading back to the academy. As the wagon began to pull away, the cadets looked back, waved, and shouted, "Thank you, Grandma!" We waved a silent good-bye in return and went back to finish our breakfast.

Through the doorway into the dining room, we could see our fathers begin to excuse themselves from the table and head out the door toward the barn. Shortly after that, we could hear the sounds of horses being hitched up to their buggies, bags being loaded and tied down, and snippets of our fathers' conversations about the weather and the drive home.

Our mothers came into the kitchen and urged us to finish our breakfast so we could get an early start home. Finishing, we got down from our chairs and walked out to the driveway. I found Father in the third buggy in line behind Mr. Porter and Mr. Hobart. I hugged each of my friends good-bye and told them I would see them at school on Monday. I then reluctantly turned back to our buggy. Mother, Elise, and I quickly climbed inside. I could see that Father had all our bags tied to the back of the buggy but had left the bag with Elise's dress under her seat.

All of a sudden, I let out a shout. "Wait, Father! I forgot Horace!" I immediately jumped down from the buggy, ran into the house, and went all the way back up to the attic, where I found Horace blissfully asleep in his box in the corner. Picking up his box, I ran back down to the kitchen and politely asked one of the kitchen girls if I might have a lettuce leaf that I could give Horace for the ride home. She nodded, smiled, and went to the icebox to get some lettuce. When she gave it to me, I said, "Thank you. Horace thanks you, too." I placed the lettuce leaf right next to him.

I quickly walked out the back door to the driveway. I watched Horace extend his long neck and head out of his shell, open his mouth wide, and chomp down on the lettuce leaf. I could just tell from what had to be a smile that he was very happy with that big green leaf of lettuce. I thanked Father for waiting, gently wedged Horace's box under my seat, and climbed back into the buggy.

Grandma and Grandpa stood at the end of their walk by the driveway, waving and telling everyone good-bye. When the Porter and Hobart families drove out of the yard, Father pulled forward and stopped at the step by Grandma and Grandpa. He and Mother said their good-byes from their seats, but Elise and I jumped down from the buggy, hugged them both, told them that we loved them, and promised that we'd be back soon. I gave Grandma an extra-long hug. She knew why!

As soon as we were settled back in the buggy, Father called out to Midnight and Storm, "Get on, you two. It's time we headed for home." As they noisily clip-clopped out of Grandma's drive, Father turned them toward the north road. Looking up the hill, Mother pointed out thick stands of tall, waving maple trees whose leaves were a sea of deep reds and bright yellows.

I really wasn't interested in trees or leaves right then, so I turned to look back at Grandma. At that exact same moment, Grandma looked at me. As our eyes met, I laughed and gave a big wave. I could see her smile as she waved back. Then she stopped waving and, still looking at me, patted the right side of her dress.

I looked at her blankly, and, for some reason, I reached down and patted my right pocket. To my surprise, wrapped in a napkin inside were two of Grandma's delicious cookies, which she'd somehow slipped into my pocket when she hugged me good-bye. I laughed again and waved one final thank-you as the buggy rounded the first bend away from Grandma's. *I think I'll share one of the cookies with Elise on the long trip home*, I thought. *She needs some cheering up.*

I settled back on the buggy seat and pulled a blanket up onto my lap. *What a wonderful visit we had at Grandma's. Elise had a fantastic debutante ball, and I had great fun spending the entire night with my friends.* Looking out at the passing trees, I smiled a blissful smile. *I love Grandma and Grandpa, and I always love coming to visit them.*

But I must admit, I also really loved the many hidden treasures that my friends and I found in Grandma's attic.

Grandma's Favorite Cookie and Cake Recipes

RAISIN AND NUT CRUMBLE COOKIES

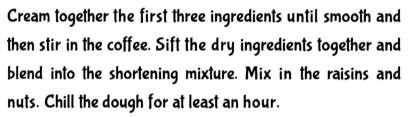

Ingredients:

- 1 cup shortening
- 2 cups brown sugar (packed)
- 2 eggs
- ½ cup cold coffee
- 3½ cups flour
- 1 teaspoon baking soda
- 1 teaspoon salt
- 1 teaspoon cinnamon
- 2½ cups raisins
- 1¼ cups chopped nuts
  (pecans or walnuts are best)

Directions:

Heat oven to 375 degrees.

Cream together the first three ingredients until smooth and then stir in the coffee. Sift the dry ingredients together and blend into the shortening mixture. Mix in the raisins and nuts. Chill the dough for at least an hour.

Drop rounded teaspoons of dough about two inches apart onto a lightly greased baking sheet (1890s version) or on parchment paper (twenty-first-century version). Bake 7 minutes or until brown on edges.

Makes 7 to 8 dozen 2½-inch cookies.

CINNAMON AND SUGAR DELIGHT COOKIES

Ingredients:

- ½ cup shortening (part butter)
- 1 cup sugar
- 1 egg
- ¾ cup buttermilk
- 1 teaspoon vanilla
- 2 cups flour
- ½ teaspoon baking soda
- ½ teaspoon salt
- ½ cup sugar
- 2 teaspoons cinnamon

Directions:

Heat oven to 400 degrees.

Cream the shortening, sugar, and egg thoroughly until smooth. Stir in the buttermilk and vanilla. Sift together the flour, soda, and salt, and blend into the creamed mixture. Chill the dough.

Mix sugar and cinnamon in a small bowl. Drop rounded teaspoons of dough into the sugar and cinnamon mixture. Coat and then place them onto a lightly greased baking sheet (1890s version) or on parchment paper (twenty-first-century version) about two inches apart. Bake 8 to 10 minutes or until set but not brown.

Makes about 4 dozen 2-inch cookies.

APPLE STREUSEL COFFEE CAKE

Ingredients:

Cake
- 1¼ cups sugar
- ½ cup soft shortening
- 2 eggs
- ¾ cup milk
- 2½ cups flour
- 3 teaspoons baking powder
- ¾ teaspoon salt
- 2 large Granny Smith apples

Streusel Mixture
- 1½ cups brown sugar (packed)
- 6 tablespoons flour
- 6 tablespoons cinnamon
- 1½ cups chopped nuts (pecans are best)
- 6 tablespoons melted butter

Directions:

Heat oven to 375 degrees.
Grease and flour a 9-by-13 metal cake pan. For the cake, start by creaming the sugar, shortening, and eggs thoroughly. Stir in the milk. Sift the dry ingredients together and stir into the wet mixture. Peel, core, and dice apples into small pieces and mix into the cake batter. In another bowl, stir streusel mixture's dry ingredients together and mix with melted butter. Spread half of the cake batter into the pan. Sprinkle half of the streusel mixture over the first half of the cake batter. Gently cover with the other half of the batter and then sprinkle the remaining streusel mixture over the top.

Bake 25–35 minutes or until a broom straw, cake tester, or toothpick comes out clean. Serve warm.

Autographs

Autographs

About the Author

Tom Frazee is an executive communications consultant with his own public relations company, CommSol, Inc. He penned this book as a complement to a highly entertaining children's ballet developed by his wife, Elaine. *Hidden Treasures in Grandma's Attic* is the first in a series of Katy and Friends adventures that will each have an original and complementing children's ballet available for performances by ballet companies and studios throughout the world. More about this first book and details on the corresponding ballet can be found at www.KatyAndFriends.com.

About the Illustrator

Britanny Zendejas is a visual artist who grew up in Los Angeles in the 90s. When she wasn't watching Saturday morning cartoons, she was drawing her own. Her style still incorporates the bold, dark outlines of these earliest influences. Britanny received her bachelor's degree in Fine Arts at Oregon State University, graduating with honors and the Distinguished Student award in her field. Since then, she has done various freelance work, been involved in local art shows, and taught art classes and community workshops in central Oregon. She currently lives in Seattle, Washington, with her partner, Andrew.